www.kindermusik.com

Written by Traci N. Todd.
Illustrations by Jesse Reisch.
Book Design by Kym Abrams Design.

ISBN 1-58987-023-9

Published in 2003 by Kindermusik International, Inc.

Do-Re-Me & You! is a trademark of Kindermusik International, Inc.

Printed in China
First printing, August 2003

# The Drum Circle

by Traci N. Todd
illustrated by Jesse Reisch

When Caleb, his dad, and Reggie arrived at the beach, the drum circle was in full swing. Caleb ran toward his friends in the circle. Together they liked to make up rhymes and chants about the different drums. When Caleb started the rhymes, the drummers knew just how to finish them.

"Mr. Bambara!" Caleb called. "What's that drum?"

"A *djembé* from Mali."

Bum–
ba–bum–
bum!

"The people of Mali know a special trick.
When they play the *djembé* drum, it soothes the sick.
Can you feel the power of the *djembé* drum?"

Then Mr. Bambara played a soothing rhythm.

# Bum-ba-bum-bum!

# bum!

Caleb closed his eyes and concentrated really hard. "I can feel the power of the *djembé* drum!" he cried. And on his own drum, Caleb played a soothing *bum-ba-bum-bum!*

"Mr. Peters!" called Caleb. "What drum is that?"

"A *dundun* from Nigeria."

Tippy- tap-

"It's also called a talking drum. It can make a sound like words.
It has to be the smartest drum that you have ever heard.
Can you hear the talking drum say your name?"

Then Mr. Peters played a talking rhythm
that sounded like Caleb's name.

Tip-tap!

**Tip-tap!**

Caleb closed his eyes and concentrated really hard. "I can hear it!" he cried. "I can hear the talking drum say my name!" And on his own drum, Caleb *tip-tapped* his name.

"Mr. Domingo!" called Caleb. "What drum is that?"

"A conga from Cuba."

PaPPY-PaP-

"You can't resist the conga drums! You have to move your feet to the rhythm of the tropics and the happy Latin beat. Can you dance to the rhythm of the conga drums?"

Then Mr. Domingo played a dancing rhythm.

Pap-pappy-
pap-pap!

Pap!

Pap!

Pap!

"Yes!" Caleb cried. "I can dance to the rhythm of the conga drums!" He twirled in the sand as he *pappy-pappy-papped* on his drum.

"Mrs. Valera!" called Caleb. "What are those things?"

"Steel drums from Trinidad."

Ping-a-
ping-ping!

"We play the drums for Carnival—what a festive sight!
We dress ourselves in costumes; we sing and dance all night!"

Then Mrs. Valera played a party rhythm.

**Ping-a-ping-Ping!**
**Ping! Ping! Ping!**

"Yes!" laughed Caleb. "I can hear the party in the steel drums!" And on his own drum, Caleb *ping-pinged* a party rhythm.

**Bum-ba-bum!**

**Tippy-tippy-tap!**

**Ping! Ping! Ping!**

**Pappy-Pap!**

**Pappy-Pap!**

Caleb and the drummers really felt the rhythms now. They were playing so hard that they didn't notice Reggie. He was racing up the beach chasing a storm of seabirds. Suddenly, hundreds of birds *whooshed* through the drum circle. The drummers were surrounded by fluttering feathers and flapping wings!

"Reggie!" cried Caleb's father.

"Look out!" shouted Mr. Bambara.

"*Aie!*" cried Mr. Domingo.

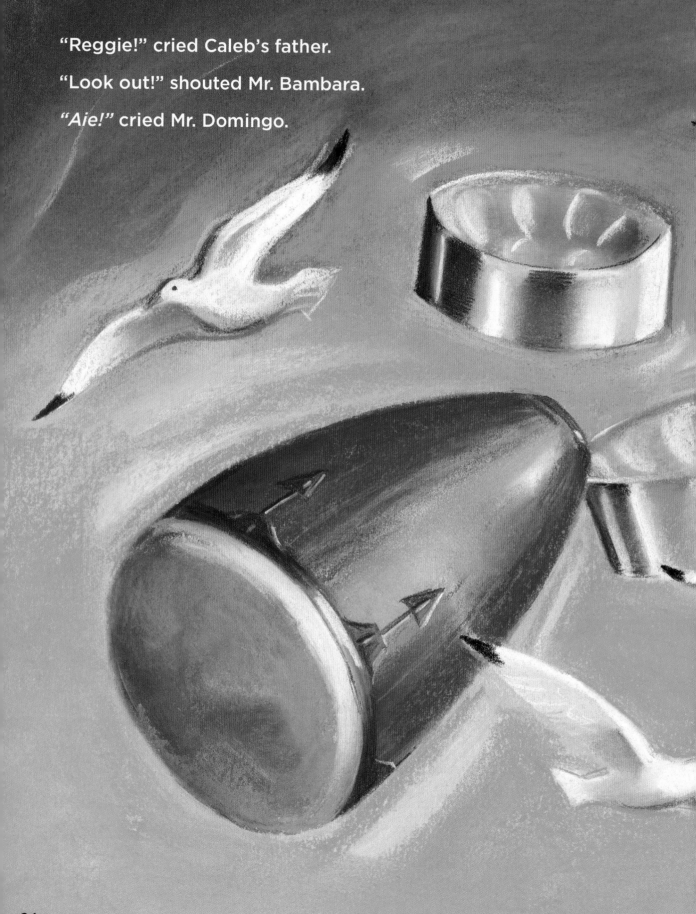

The drummers ducked and covered their heads, throwing their many drums high into the air. Up went Mr. Bambara's *djembé*. Up went Mr. Domingo's congas. Up went Mrs. Valera's steel drums. Up, up, up!

Then down came the congas in front of Mr. Peters.
Down came the *djembé* in front of Mr. Domingo.
Down came the steel drums in front of Mr. Bambara.
No one had the right drum.

Caleb and his dad frowned at Reggie.
Reggie looked very sorry.

Then something wonderful happened. Mr. Bambara picked up the steel drums and played a soft, soothing rhythm. Mr. Domingo played a dancing rhythm on the *djembé*, and Mr. Peters *tap-tippy-tapped* on the congas. Each drum sounded very different than it had before, but the new sounds were just right.

From that day on, when the drum circle met on the beach, the drummers played each other's drums. They taught each other new rhythms, and Caleb made up new rhymes. And because Reggie inspired this new drum-circle tradition, he was always welcome.

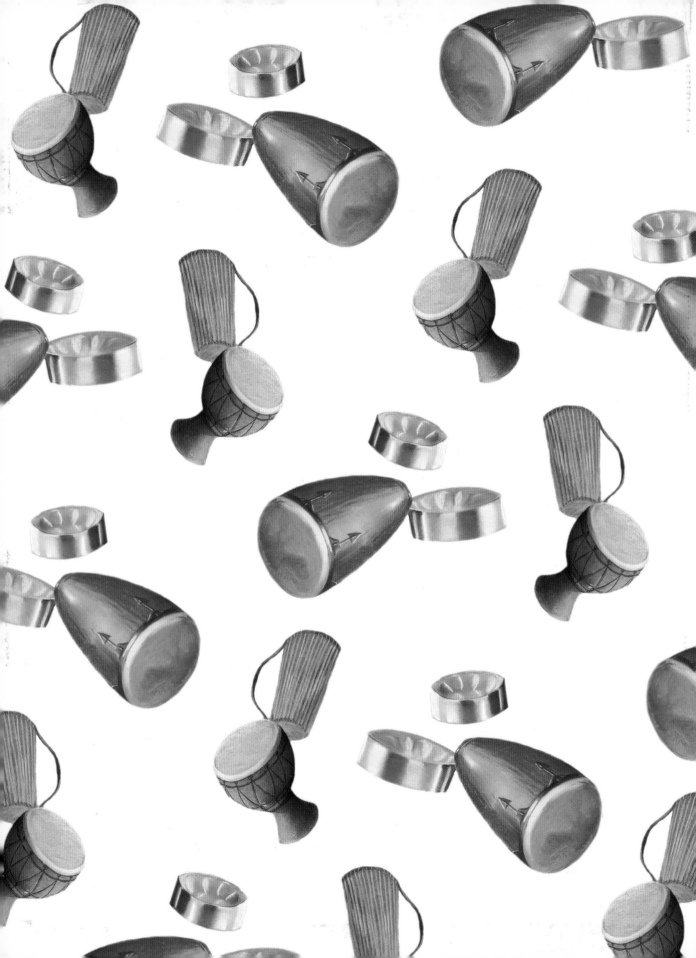